Pump!

A novel by

Sharon Jennings

HIP-JR.

HIP Junior
Copyright © 2006 by Sharon Jennings

Library and Archives Canada Cataloguing in Publication

Jennings, Sharon
    Pump! / Sharon Jennings.

(HIP jr)
ISBN 1-897039-19-0

I. Title. II. Series.

PS8569.E563P86 2006   jC813'.54   C2006-903374-9

General editor: Paul Kropp
Text design and typesetting: Laura Brady
Illustrations drawn by: Catherine Doherty
Cover design: Robert Corrigan

1 2 3 4 5 6 7   06 07 08 09 10

Printed and bound in Canada

High Interest Publishing is an imprint of the
Chestnut Publishing Group

Pump: a way to gain energy and speed.

Enter the half pipe in a crouch. Then rise to a standing position as you start the upward slope.

Erin
marie Eric

CHAPTER 1

Grinding Away

So how did I get into this life or death mess?

I guess it started the day I skipped school. I was outside my house, ready to try a couple of things with my skateboard. I lit a whole book of matches and held them under a candle. As soon as the candle was soft, I spread the wax along the curb. Then I grabbed my board. I ran up the driveway and hopped on. I wanted to try out my goofyfoot for a change.

When I did a quick turn, my trucks slid on the

candle wax. I did a grind along the curb and ollied back onto the sidewalk. Thunk! Then I did a manual along the sidewalk and an acid-drop off the curb. Thunk!

I kept at it, over and over. That's what a real pro would do. You can't get better if you don't practice. I had the whole afternoon to work on my line.

Down the driveway, turn, grind. Over and over and over. Thunk! Thunk! Thunk! I knew I was getting better. I could hardly wait to show Ryan when he got home from school.

Then I tried my ollie again and got just a little bit more air. Sweet.

Yeah, real sweet, until I saw Mrs. Harris come flying out of her house.

"Shut up," she screamed. "You know my kids are napping."

As if her screaming wouldn't wake up the kids.

So I held my finger up to my lips. "Shhhh!" I said.

"I guess you think you're pretty funny," she yelled. She flicked ash from her cigarette which fell down at my feet.

"No ma'am," I said. "But if your kids are asleep, why are you yelling so much?"

"Because I'm sick of listening to you and your stupid skateboard. The noise is driving me crazy and. . . ." She stopped talking and got right in my face. I could smell the smoke on her breath. "Why aren't you in school, Patrick?"

"It's my lunch hour," I said. Then I added her name. "Mrs. Harris."

"It's two o'clock," she answered. "Lunch is over."

"Yeah, well, I had a spare."

"You're in grade 7. You don't get spares."

How did she know so much? I didn't say anything. I looked at the ground.

"Well, well, well. I knew you were a loser. You're skipping school!"

I sighed and rolled my eyes.

"Your mom can't control you. Maybe I should call Children's Aid."

I smiled at that. "Why don't you?" I said to her. "Ask for my mom. That's where she works."

"Really?" replied Mrs. Harris. "Well, it just goes to show. She can't control her own brat but she's a do-gooder for the rest of the world."

"Don't you say anything about my mom!" I yelled. I took a step toward her.

Mrs. Harris backed away. Then she pointed to the curb. "Look at that mess. Maybe I should just call the cops."

Then she turned and headed back to her house. She took a last drag on her cigarette and tossed it into the gutter.

Yeah. Like a cigarette butt is way better than a little wax on a curb.

And what was she doing smoking near two little kids, anyway? Hadn't she heard about second-hand smoke? Maybe I should call the cops on her!

I had dinner ready when my mom got home from work. I wasn't doing this because I thought I might get in trouble. If I'm home, I start dinner. I like cooking, that's all. Some of my friends called me Patricia when they found out. They said I was a girl. But I beat one of them up and the teasing stopped. Besides, when my friends come over, they know I can feed them.

My mom smiled when she saw me working in the kitchen.

"Smells great, Pat," she said, giving me a hug. "What are we having?"

"Pat's Parmesan Pasta," I told her.

I made up this one myself. You crack a couple of fresh eggs into a big bowl. Then add lots of parmesan cheese and bacon. Stir it up. Then toss in some cooked pasta and you're done.

I opened a bag of ready-to-go salad and found a bottle of salad dressing in the fridge. A full dinner in no time. How hard is that? You don't have to be a girl to cook.

My mom and I sat down, and I told her about Mrs. Harris.

Mom sighed and rubbed her eyes. "Pat, why did you skip school?"

"It was just gym. You know how much I hate gym," I answered.

And I did. I couldn't stand being in the change

room with all the guys, putting on our dumb outfits. I hated all the team stuff we did. I'm the guy who always gets picked last for a team. I just wanted be outside, on my board. Why can't we have skateboarding in school? Why can't we get some really famous boarder to come and teach us a few tricks? Man! I'd get an A+ for sure!

"Are you mad at me?" I asked.

My mom smiled. "A little," she said. "I'll have to phone the school tomorrow. And I'm not sure what to do about Mrs. Harris. I'll either have to dodge her or punch her in the nose."

I had to laugh. I knew my mom wouldn't hit anybody. Ever. But it was funny thinking about it. I bit the top half off a piece of pasta.

"Look," I said, holding it up. "A half pipe."

"Hey!" my mom exclaimed. "I almost forgot. On my way home from work I saw a pile of building stuff out on the curb. Just over on Elm Street. There was lots of old wood and some pipes. I thought of you as soon as I saw the pipes. I figured that...."

But I was way ahead of her.

"Wow!" I jumped up. "Thanks, Mom! I gotta tell Ryan!"

CHAPTER 2

Our Ramp

Ryan lives down my street. I ran to his house and banged on the door.

"Come on!" I yelled. "Grab your wagon!"

"What's going on?" Ryan asked.

"There's some building going on at Elm Street. There's wood and pipes and stuff. We've got to get over there and grab everything before someone else does."

Ryan knew exactly what I was planning.

"A ramp!" Ryan yelled. He ran to the garage for his little sister's wagon.

We got to Elm in seconds and looked up and down the street. We saw a pile of junk on the curb a few houses down and hurried over. I couldn't believe all the stuff that was there. I grabbed a few pipes. Ryan hauled out big sheets of wood.

"Oh, man!" said Ryan. "This is like finding treasure! We can build the ramp just like we always wanted to!"

I nodded. I had lots of plans and drawings at home. One day, I wanted to build a mega ramp — something that Danny Way would want to ride. But for now, a one-metre launch ramp with a rail would be just perfect.

I smiled at Ryan.

"Sweet," I said.

Ryan and I dumped everything in the shed behind my house. I ran inside for a saw, a hammer and nails.

"So what are we going to build?" Ryan asked.

"A vert ramp would be cool," I said.

Ryan nodded.

A vert ramp is usually about three metres high. I didn't think we were going to get that high with the stuff we found.

"Have you ever done vert boarding?" Ryan asked.

I shook my head. "It'd be awesome," I said.

Making a ramp is trickier than it seems. We hammered and sawed and called each other idiots a lot. I guess we were making a lot of noise. This old guy who lives behind my house heard us and stared over the fence.

"Oh, great," I said. "Now one more neighbour's going to complain."

But I was wrong.

"What are you building?" asked the old guy.

"A ramp," I mumbled.

"A ramp, eh? For skateboarding?"

"Yeah," I said. I kept my back to him.

"My grandson made one of those," the old guy went on. "Want a little advice?"

Well, we did and we didn't. We wanted to make

the ramp all by ourselves, but we wanted it to work. Like right away. So I said "yeah" and the old guy came over.

He showed us how to steady the supports so our ramp wasn't lopsided. And then he showed us how to attach the pipes along the side of the ramp.

When that was done, I smiled and stuck out my hand.

"Thanks, Mister. . . ."

"Mr. Perez," he said.

"Thanks a lot, Mr. Perez," I said. "You want to try it out when we're done?"

The old guy laughed. "I don't think my knees would like that. But I wouldn't mind watching you. Seems like fun."

He shook my hand and went back around the fence.

"That guy sure makes up for Mrs. Harris," I told Ryan. "Not all of my neighbors are jerks."

We finished the ramp just as it was getting dark. We hauled it down my driveway and out onto the street.

"You go first," said Ryan.

So I grabbed my board and manualed down the drive. I did a backside 180 off the ramp and flew through the air. I went about two metres before touching down.

Thunk!

"Oh, man!" I shouted. "This is sweet! This is the best!"

Ryan got on his board and did the same line.

Thunk!

He pumped his fist in the air and laughed.

So we went again and again, taking turns. We both fell a lot, especially when we tried grinding the pipes. That is one hard trick!

I figured I'd give it one more try. Down the driveway, quick turn, up the ramp and WHAM! Maybe I was tired. Maybe I was stupid. But my wheels missed the ramp and off I flew. I smashed down on the pavement. Hard.

Next thing I knew, my mom was running down the sidewalk. She was screaming.

And a cop car was coming up the street.

CHAPTER 3

A Close Call

When a cop is sitting in his car, he looks like a normal guy. When he gets out of his car, he looks really, really big. And scary. But not half as scary as my mom jumping up and down in front of me.

"You alright?" asked the cop.

"Um, yeah, um, I think," I mumbled.

"No, he's not alright," yelled my mom. "How can he be alright when he's bleeding?"

"Ah, Mom. It was just a little fall," I said. "It

happens all the time." Besides, I wasn't bleeding that much.

That really got my mom going. "Are you trying to kill yourself?" she began. Then she really let me have it.

It took the cop to stop her. "Now, now," said the cop. "Time you went inside, kid. I had a complaint about the noise."

I looked up at Mrs. Harris's house. I saw a curtain move a bit and then drop down again.

Suddenly, my mom stopped glaring at me.

"Who complained?" she asked.

"Just a neighbour, ma'am," said the cop. "No big deal. Did all those other kids take off? I heard there was a gang out here using this ramp. Where did your friends go?" asked the cop.

"There wasn't anybody else. Just us," I said.

The cop looked like he didn't believe me.

"It's true," said my mom. "No one else was here but Ryan and Pat."

"Well, how about calling it a night?" said the cop. "It's getting a little late. Some folks are trying to get their kids to sleep."

"Sure," I said. "Come on, Ryan. Let's put the ramp away."

"Wait a minute," said the cop. "Did you make this ramp yourselves?"

"Yeah," I answered. "Well, most of it."

"Can you show me a trick before I go?" he asked.

"You mean, like, teach you?" I asked.

The cop laughed. "No. Just show me what you can do."

Seemed pretty weird — a cop asking to see some tricks. But what the heck. Ryan and I both did a couple of good ones.

I guess Mrs. Harris was watching from her window and couldn't figure out what was going on. I bet she wanted the cop to arrest us. Instead, he was being nice.

She slammed her front door shut and marched over to us.

"I hope you told these two little losers to stop the racket," Mrs. Harris demanded.

"Things are taken care of, ma'am," said the cop.

"It doesn't look like it," said Mrs. Harris.

"Did you call the cops?" asked my mother. "Did you lie about how many kids were here?"

"Now everybody keep calm," said the cop. "The boys are shutting down for the night."

"But what about tomorrow? Do I have to listen to this racket all day?" asked Mrs. Harris.

"They're just kids," said my mom.

"They're losers," said Mrs. Harris.

"Listen," said my mom. "I work with kids all day who don't remember how to play. Kids who are beaten up by their parents. Kids who have no toys. Kids who go to school hungry." She stopped for a second. "I'm sick of people who can't stand to see kids have a little fun!"

Mrs. Harris didn't say anything. She blew some smoke in my mom's face and walked away.

My mom looked like she wanted to run after her. She looked like she wanted to punch Mrs. Harris in the nose! But I knew she wouldn't. My mom sees too many people fighting all day long.

That's why she'd never hit anybody. It makes her sick to think about it.

"Whew!" said the cop. "I'm glad I don't have *her* for a neighbour!"

My mom let out a deep sigh. "Oh, well. Live and let live," she said.

"So how about if you boys just be a little careful?" asked the cop. "Don't skateboard after dark. Don't make too much noise. Take a break every now and then."

Ryan and I nodded. I mean, we have to eat and go to the bathroom and watch TV. Sure. We could take breaks.

So the cop shook our hands and then he gave me his card. His name was Officer Burns.

"Keep cool," he said. "And call me any time if there's a problem. Okay?"

Ryan and I nodded again.

We watched him drive off, and then we hauled our ramp back up the driveway.

Then I made sure I locked the shed door. I didn't want Mrs. Harris getting any ideas.

CHAPTER 4

Go With the Flow

At school the next day, we told everyone about our ramp. A whole bunch of guys wanted to come over and give it a try.

"Sure," I said. "It'll be cool."

So right after school a bunch of us headed over to my house. We got out the ramp and started taking turns. Everybody wanted to show off their stuff.

A couple of kids were posers. They had the best skateboards and all the expensive equipment, but they couldn't even manual the sidewalk without tripping. This one kid was really clutzy, but he was cool. He kept trying and trying no matter how many times he fell.

We all quit a bit for supper, and then everyone came back. Someone brought this older kid. I didn't know him, but I'd heard about him. His nickname was Bird and he was in grade nine. Some other kids showed up just to watch. Then I saw Mr. Perez come along on a bicycle. He waved to us and pulled over.

"Mind if I watch?" he asked.

I smiled. "Hey! It's half your ramp."

Soon we got into a routine. We took turns, one after another. Cruise along the street, then do your best trick off the ramp.

Some kids were great. They could do kickflips no problem. I watched Bird fly through the air. It was like his board was magic. He didn't lose it once. I figured out why his nickname was Bird.

"How do you do that?" I asked.

He just shrugged. "You've got to stay loose. No tension, man. Just go with the flow."

So I tried to copy him, keeping my legs loose. I kept dropping my board.

"Not bad," Bird said. "But you've really got to bend the knees. It's all in the knees. Really push down when you want to go up."

Huh?

"It's all about force and momentum," Bird went on. "It's cool."

I didn't get what he was talking about. So he showed me again. As he was about to go off the ramp, he suddenly did this deep knee bend.

"Push down!" he shouted. Then he brought his knees up to his chest. Up he flew into the air, his skateboard looking like it was glued to his feet.

So we all tried it.

"Push! Push! Push!" he yelled at us over and over.

Thunk! Thunk! Thunk!

Well, we were working so hard, and having so much fun, we didn't see how late it was.

And we didn't notice the cop car until it was on top of us.

"Ah, man," I said. "Not again."

Officer Burns got out of the car.

"Sorry, boys," said Officer Burns. "Break it up."

"But you said it was alright," I said to him.

Officer Burns sighed.

"We got a whole bunch of complaints tonight. You're making too much noise. A couple of your neighbors said you were swearing and blocking the road."

"Ah, man," I said again. "We were just having fun. We're not bothering anybody."

"There's a bylaw that says you can't play on the street," said Officer Burns.

"Yeah. We know all about it," said Ryan. "That same bylaw says we can't play street hockey. The city has bylaws against lots of stuff."

"Sorry, kids," replied Officer Burns. "The neighbors have got a real complaint, so there's not much I can do. You'll just have to skateboard someplace else."

He got back into the cruiser and drove off.

I slammed my board down.

"Where else do we go?" I asked. "There's no skateboarding park around here. And if we go to the school playground, we get chased out of there, too."

But then Mr. Perez said, "The city is talking about building a park for you kids. A skateboarding park. I hear they've picked a spot in Hillside Park. It was in the paper last week. But it's not a sure thing yet."

"How come I didn't know about this?" I asked. I was excited but didn't want it to show.

"Cause you can't read," said Ryan.

I punched his arm.

"There's going to be a meeting soon," said Mr. Perez. "The mayor will be there. Anyone can go. Anyone can have their say."

"What's there to say?" asked Ryan. "We'll all go and tell the mayor we want a park!"

"Yeah, right," I said. "You know what'll happen? A bunch of old farts will show up and stop them from building the park. No one wants kids hanging out, having a good time."

"I guess you think I'm an old fart," said Mr. Perez.

"Oops. Sorry," I said.

"But I support this park," said Mr. Perez. "Why don't you all find out about the meeting and go? Why don't you make sure the park gets built?"

"You think we have a chance?" I asked.

"Tell you what," said Mr. Perez. "If you go to the meeting, I'll go, too. Deal?"

I looked around at the other kids. I looked over at Mrs. Harris's window. Then I looked at my useless ramp.

"Deal," I said.

But Bird had another idea.

"And what if some of us don't want a park?" he asked. "What if I'd rather skate the streets? What if I don't buy into this whole skate-in-the-park thing?"

Mr. Perez just looked at him.

"What if you just lead the way and we all go look at the site?" Mr. Perez said.

Seemed like a plan.

CHAPTER 5

Dying to Vert

Off we went, all of us on our boards . . . and Mr. Perez on his bike.

Hillside Park isn't very far from my house. We were there in only ten minutes. The only other skateboarding park in my town is about an hour away by car. I've been there twice. So a place this close would be totally cool. I could board every day if my mom let me.

We went through and around the park to the southeast corner. It was an empty parking lot. Some kids were boarding there already.

"The city picked this place because no one ever parks their cars here," said Mr. Perez. "But kids come here to board so it seemed like a good idea."

Then he took us over to a notice board. Plans for the park were posted. They looked awesome!

The park would be done up street style. There would be stairs, curbs, ledges and handrails. There would be some kickers and even a half pipe. Not quite up to Danny Way's standards, but pretty good for us.

Then Mr. Perez said, "They're going to install a video system here. If somebody gets hurt, the camera will pick it up."

"That sucks," said Bird. "That's just so the cops can spy on us."

Some of the other kids agreed with him.

"But this is how you can convince the city that the park is a safe place," replied Mr. Perez.

"How do you know so much?" I asked.

"I told you my grandson boards. When I found out there might be a park around here, I looked into it. When he visits me, I can bring him here."

Then he hopped on his bike and rode off.

"See you around, boys. Don't forget what I said."

We all stood around talking. It was getting pretty late. My mom would be wondering where I was. I was all set to head home, but Bird had another idea.

"Who wants to have some fun?" he asked.

"What do you mean?" I said.

"Follow me and find out," he said. "Or do you all want to bail?"

No one wanted to be called a chicken. One by one, we hopped on our boards and followed him out of the parking lot.

We went back through the park, chasing after Bird. He finally stopped in front of the swimming pool. It wasn't filled yet for summer. Each end of the pool was a shallow end, with slopes going down to the deep middle.

"So who's up for vert skating?" Bird called.

You've got to be kidding, I thought. But he wasn't. Bird was over the fence and grinding down

the steps to the pool. We all just watched him as he rode up the sides.

He shouted out to us. "This is what boarding is all about. We take over public space. We don't wait for somebody to say it's okay. We don't need parks. Be a rebel. Don't sell out!"

Sounded good to us. We all hopped the fence.

Vert skating looks easy. That's because you have to be a great skater to try it. A great skater makes everything look cool.

But Ryan and I sucked. No one was anywhere near Bird. I watched him pump. He came down one side of the pool in a low crouch. Then he stood straight up and went faster and faster. He flew up the other side and even did a method grab as he cleared the pool.

I wanted to try it, I really did. But, well, an empty pool is pretty scary.

Then that's when some kid called me a poser. That's when I tried to tailslide the lip of the pool. That's when I fell. That's when I passed out.

Or died.

CHAPTER 6

You're Done!

The bright light was shining into my eyes.

The next thing I knew I was being rushed to a hospital. And then a whole bunch of people were doing a whole bunch of things to my body.

But then came the very worst part. My mother showed up.

She hugged me and then started yelling.

"Why weren't you wearing your helmet? Where were you? I ought to punch you in the nose!"

When the doctor came in, she told us I needed

six stitches. I had a big gash on the back of my head.

"This won't hurt," the doc said.

Then she made me lie face down. They shaved a spot on my head and froze the area with something cold. When she told me I could sit up, I didn't get it.

"When are you doing the stitches?" I asked.

"They're done, Pat. Your stitches are all done," she told me.

So I started to put on my shoes and take off my hospital gown. But my mom told me to sit down. She wanted to know exactly what happened.

I told her all about going to the park.

"And Mr. Perez was with us the whole time," I said. I thought that would make her feel better.

It didn't.

"Pat, I work with kids all day who have been in bad accidents. You know you should have been wearing your helmet. You know what can happen. How many times do I have to tell you. . . ."

"Aw, Mom. Come on. I'm fine. The doctor said

so. I'll be back on my board by tomorrow."

"Tomorrow?" my mom shrieked. "You think I'll ever let you skateboard again? Ever? Are you nuts?! You had two accidents in two days!"

"Mom," I told her, "you can't stop me boarding. You can't. It's my life!"

My mom would have kept going, but the doctor came back in to check on me. In a few minutes, she said I could go home. She even said I should stay home from school the next day.

But my mom had other plans. She made me go to work with her.

My mom works all over the city. She checks up on kids who have been abused, so she's always on the go. But sometimes she goes to this hospital for kids who have been badly hurt. Some of the kids are in this place for years.

That's where she took me.

She introduced me to this kid named John. He was one of her clients in foster care, but then he got hit by a drunk driver. He was on his bike and wasn't wearing a helmet. A bad call. No matter what the doctors did, John would never walk again. He'd be stuck in a wheelchair for the rest of his life.

I felt kind of weird talking to the guy. John was in here for the long haul because of what happened. I was here for one day because I had a bump on my head. But John wanted to know what happened to me, so I told him. Then he told me to follow him back to his room. His walls were covered with posters of Danny Way and Tony Hawk.

"I love watching boarders," he said. "I wish I could still do it."

"Yeah, well, I won't be skateboarding much if we don't get this park built. My mom is ready to nail my board to the wall."

So I told him about the ramp, and I told him about Mrs. Harris.

"It seems only fair you should have a park," John said. "I mean, old folks take up half the city with their golf courses."

"Hey, you're right," I said. "But golfers don't upset the neighbors. So no one cares."

"Someone should care," said John. "That's who hit me. A guy who had a bad round of golf and started drinking. Got in his car half drunk — and then ran into me."

"I'm sorry, man," I said. "Really sorry."

"Ah, forget it," John shrugged. "So how long have you been boarding?"

"Two years," I said.

"Are you any good?" he asked.

"I'm not great," I said. "But I'm not a poser, if

that's what you mean."

"I watch the boarding shows on TV all the time," said John. "I like to pretend that one day I'll do all those tricks."

"Me too," I replied. Then I remembered something. "You know, Danny Way broke his neck a few years ago. He was skating again a year later. It could happen for you too, man," I said.

But John didn't answer me. He just stared out the window. Then without looking at me, he said, "Did you bring your board with you? I'd like to see your stuff."

"I can't. My mom's still hot about me not wearing my helmet yesterday."

When my mom came to get me, I said goodbye to John.

He yelled after me as I went down the hall. "If you come back again, Pat, bring your board. Lots of kids here would watch you."

"Sure," I replied.

I rode home in the car with my mom. I knew what she wanted to hear.

"Mom, I know I was wrong last night. I know you don't want me to end up in a wheelchair. I promise to wear my helmet from now on and I mean it."

My mom smiled. "John's a great kid," she said.

I nodded. "Do you think he really wants me to come back?"

"Why not?" said my mom.

"Do you think he really wants me to bring my skateboard?"

"You heard him. John doesn't say anything he doesn't mean," replied my mom.

And that got me thinking.

Why would a kid in a wheelchair want to see a guy skateboarding? Wouldn't that kind of thing bother him?

So I did some more thinking. I like watching hockey and baseball and I suck at those sports. But I don't hate the players. I mean, some of them are awesome and it makes me feel good to watch them. I don't get jealous.

So maybe it was like that for John. Maybe it

made him feel good watching skateboarders. I mean, why else would he have their posters up on his wall?

So I decided I'd go back to visit John, and I'd bring my board.

Then I thought some more. Maybe I'd bring some of my friends. Maybe there was a place we could really do our stuff. Maybe we could put on a real show. I mean, if those kids wanted to watch, why not?

It wasn't like Mrs. Harris wanted to watch me.

CHAPTER 7

Internet Rescue

The next day, I felt good enough to go back to school. A few kids pointed at my shaved head and yelled "Spazz!" But my friends were cool. I saw Bird as he crossed to the high school.

"You ain't a good boarder if you don't have scars," he told me.

That made me feel good. But I decided not to tell that to my mom. I didn't think she'd see it that way.

At lunch, I got my friends together.

"So are we going to go for this park or what?" I asked.

"What do you mean?" said Ryan.

"You heard Mr. Perez," I said. "Are we going to fight for what we want or not?"

"What can we do?" someone asked.

"First, we find out about the meeting," I told them. "Then we find out how we get to have our say. Then we make sure we say something good. There's no way Mrs. Harris is ruining my life."

Well, we all wanted a park, but nobody had any good ideas. Then I remembered what Mr. Perez said. He'd told us the police liked the idea of a boarder park. The cops would rather know where we're boarding than have to guess. So I thought I'd call Officer Burns and ask for his help.

I made dinner for my mom that night. While we ate, I told her what I wanted to do. She surprised me. I mean, I was ready for a real hard time. But she just sighed and rolled her eyes.

"Do I want you to skateboard? No," she sighed. "Will that stop you? No. Would you be safer in a

park? Maybe." My mom does that some times. She asks a question, then answers it herself. "So how do you pull this off? You use the Internet."

"Huh?"

"Use the Internet. Do a search on 'skateboarding, opposition.' Something like that. Lots of people hate skateboarding. Maybe you'll learn something useful. You won't get a park if you don't do some work."

So that night I got on the computer.

My mom was right. People complained any

time kids tried to put in a park. I read about lots of town meetings and what went on. I learned kids get shouted down at these meetings. No one wants to hear from us.

I learned people complain about noise even when a park is nowhere near their homes.

I learned people worry about stuff like safety and garbage. And — get this — where kids will go to the bathroom!

I learned people think all skateboarders are trash. *Trash!* That really made me mad.

So I learned three other things: I learned I wasn't going to keep quiet. I learned I was going to fight for the park! And I learned that sometimes — just sometimes — the kids could win.

So my next step was more research. I grabbed Ryan and off we went to the park.

"Okay," I said, handing him paper and a pen. "Write everything down."

I looked around and started talking.

"The boarder park is in a corner of the park no one uses. It's not close to the tennis court, the pool

or the playground. So we won't bother anyone."

I looked around some more.

"There aren't any houses nearby, just lots of traffic. So no one can complain about noise. And we're down the hill from the traffic, so cars can't hit us."

"This is good stuff," said Ryan. He kept writing away.

"There's lots of trees, too," I said. "That's good for shade. Plus they keep down noise."

I walked over to the notice board and looked at

the plans.

"They put in a washroom," I said. "And a drinking fountain. And look! They're putting in bright lights for night boarding. See? We'll all be safe."

"This place is perfect," said Ryan. "I don't see how anyone can be against it."

"But they are," I replied.

"Of course they are," Ryan answered. "But now we can fight back."

When I got home, I took out the card Officer Burns had given me. I phoned his number, and I left a message. A few minutes later he called me back. I told him about the park and about our plans.

"Good for you, Pat!" he said. "I'll see you at the meeting. I've got a few things to say. Maybe you can say something, too. . . ."

Oh no. No way! I don't ever stand up ever and talk. I don't even answer questions in class. When I try to talk in front of people, something weird happens to my stomach. Not to mention a few other body parts. I mean, I did all the research. Someone else could do the talking.

I even did more than that. I made up a bunch of flyers. Ryan and I handed them out to all the kids at school. We stuck them on posts around the neighbourhood. We stood on corners and outside stores and handed them out to every kid we saw.

"Read this," we said. "Come to the meeting next Thursday."

I'd done all I had to do. Right?

CHAPTER 8

Facing the Mob

It was Thursday. Do or die day. I went to school, but I didn't learn a thing. I made dinner for my mom and me, but I didn't eat much. Then I got up to go.

"Good luck," my mom said.

"You aren't coming?!" I shouted.

"Can't," she said. "I have to see a client."

Great. Just great. Thanks a bunch, Mom! Just when I needed all the friendly adults I can find, she takes off on me.

So I called on Ryan. Just like we planned, we met up with our friends in front of our school. About fifty kids were there. They were all holding onto their skateboards.

"Let's go," I said. "We can do this!"

"Yeah!" everyone shouted back.

We boarded our way over to the high school. A lot of people were already there. So was Officer Burns, just like he promised.

All of us boarders went in, holding onto our skateboards. We weren't acting up. We weren't even making noise. But right away, I knew there was going to be trouble. This old guy came up to me. He jabbed his finger into my chest.

"You're nothing but a punk!" he said.

He looked like he was going to hit me. But then Officer Burns was standing beside me.

"Take your seat," he said to the old guy. "Right now, sir."

Cops can sure sound tough when they want to.

We all sat down together near the front of the room. Officer Burns took the seat beside me. When the meeting finally started, the place was packed.

Someone stood up and started talking.

"Money has been put in the city budget to build a skateboarding park," he said. "After months of study, we have finally found the place for a park." He pointed to a map. "The southeast corner of Hillside Park. We're here tonight to listen to what you people have to say."

Well, he hardly finished his sentence when lots of people jumped up. They all started shouting.

"Punks!" "Druggies!" "No good teenagers!"

"Order! Order!" yelled the man at the front.

When the crowd settled down, Officer Burns got up. He faced the crowd.

"Ladies and gentlemen," he began. "Like it or not, skateboarding is here to stay." There was noise from the crowd, but Office Burns kept on. "It's big business. Kids enjoy it. We want to move kids out of parking lots and off the street. We want to give them a safe place to play. We want to protect our young people *and* your property. That's why the police are all for building this park. This can be a win-win, folks. You just have to let it go ahead."

All us kids cheered as Officer Burns finished. He sure made a lot of sense.

But not too many of the adults thought so. They kept yelling and grumbling. Then an old guy got up and warned about noise and kids hanging out. The adults all agreed with him. It looked like they had five more old guys ready to speak against the park.

But the guy at the front looked over at all of us

with our skateboards. Then he looked right at me.

"Son," he said, "why don't you come up here and tell us why you support the park."

Huh? Me?!

What was I going to say?! And how could I say anything? My mouth was dry and my tongue was thick.

But Officer Burns took my arm and sort of helped me to my feet. And all of my friends started clapping. My feet felt really heavy, but I made my way to the front.

I stood on the platform and stared at this group of angry faces. I bet this is what a mob looks like just before they run you out of town. I cleared my throat a few times and didn't know what to say. Then I looked over at all the kids who came to the meeting. I didn't want to let them down.

So I pulled one of our flyers out of my pocket and began to read. At first, my voice sounded real thin. But then, for some weird reason, I thought of Bird pumping at the pool. I saw him rise from a crouch to standing, just to gain speed and energy. I

saw him pump! Well, I couldn't do it on my board. But maybe I needed to try a little pumping to save the park.

So I took a very deep breath. Then one by one I made my points. After each point, my friends cheered. When I was done, the man at the front said, "Very good, son."

I nodded and smiled. Then I said, "I wish all of you would just let us have some fun. Maybe if you'd watch us instead of complaining about us, you'd see what it's all about."

"It's about you skipping school and bothering the neighbors!" a woman shouted. I looked over. It was Mrs. Harris.

I tried to say something more but all the adults were shouting.

Well, not all the adults. I saw Mr. Perez making his way up to the front of the room.

"Folks! Folks!" he said. "Let's calm down. We're supposed to be the adults here, remember?" That got them to quiet down. "And remember back to when you were a kid. We were all young once. We've all got kids or grandkids. Come on, folks. Let the kids have their park. Live and let live!"

"Drop dead!" Mrs. Harris shouted. *Nice*, Mrs. Harris, *real nice*.

All the adults and kids were shouting. But for me, the meeting was over. I grabbed my skateboard and headed for the door.

CHAPTER 9

What Life Is All About

I walked down the aisle, looking at so many angry faces. Why were they so angry? What did I ever do to them? What's wrong with adults?

I had just about walked out when the door opened. Someone was pushing it open with her back. When the person turned around, I saw it was my mother. She was pushing a wheelchair.

It was my buddy John.

"Hi, Pat!" he said. "Did I miss anything good?"

"What are you doing here?" I asked. "What's going on?"

"I wanted to come to the meeting," John answered. "Your mom said she'd bring me."

"But why?"

"I like skateboarding. I want you guys to get this park," John said.

Just then, someone tapped me on the shoulder. It was the man leading the meeting.

"Pat, I'd like you to come back up front. You made some good points. Now people here get to debate with you. You get to argue back. That's the way this whole thing works. You can't just walk away."

I shook my head. "No way," I said. "I've had enough. . . ."

But then I got a brainwave. I grabbed John's wheelchair.

"Come on," I said to him. "I need some help."

I pushed John to the front and turned him around to face the crowd. I didn't have time to be scared. I didn't even have to think about what I was going to say.

"This is my friend John," I shouted out. "He was hit by a drunk driver. Some guy had a lousy golf game. He got drunk and got in his car. And now John's in a wheelchair — like, for the rest of his life. My buddy wasn't hurt by a skateboarder. He was hurt by an adult. An adult like all of you."

It went very quiet in the hall.

"And here's the thing. He's not mad at me 'cause I can skateboard and he can't. He just wants to watch me. He has fun watching boarders do their stuff."

Then John asked me for the mike. I had to take it off the stand and hand it down.

John cleared his throat and looked at the adults. "I used to love skateboarding," he said. "It's all about the feeling you get when you're catching air. It's about the feeling when you do something that looks impossible. I used to do that stuff. I used to love to do that stuff. But now I love watching other guys go for it. I wouldn't take that away from them. Why would you?"

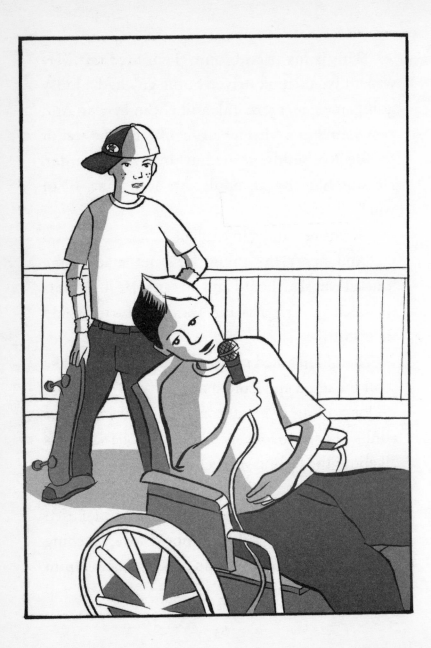

The crowd grew silent. I think they were embarrassed.

"You've got fifty kids here who just want a skateboard park," John went on. "They don't want to hang out on street corners. They don't want to smash their heads skating on a driveway. They just want to have some good, safe fun. Is that too much to ask?" He let the question hang in the air. "No," John said, "it's not much at all. Let them build the park!"

All of a sudden, my friends stood up and pumped their skateboards in the air. Then some of the adults stood up and started clapping.

After a few minutes, the man leading the meeting called for order. It took a long time for people to settle down.

"I think we've learned a lot tonight," he said. "And it seems pretty simple to me. The people who don't want the park have not had much to offer."

We all cheered one more time!

The meeting continued, but I didn't have to talk again. Stuff was argued back and forth, but

Officer Burns was in there the whole time. He kept speaking up for our park. So did John. So did my mom.

At ten, the meeting was called to an end. We all headed for the snack table. I got juice and cookies for John and me.

"Now what?" I asked him. "Does my mom have to take you back home?"

"Not until I get what I came for," John replied.

I didn't know what he meant.

"The show, stupid," he said. "I want to see your line. Or maybe you really are a poser." He was grinning and I grinned back.

"You got it," I said. "Come on, guys!" I called to my friends.

I took John out to the playground. The big lights were still on, so it was perfect for a skateboard show.

I started off. First I ollied the stairs and did a few acid-drops off a curb. A couple of kids did a grind down the railings. Lots of people had stopped to watch us. Soon, a big circle formed and

all of us guys performed in the middle. It wasn't just kids. Adults were there, too, cheering and clapping. Then Bird showed up and showed us again why he was called Bird. He climbed to the top of the slide, used it as a launch and flew up into the air. He stayed there like he was never coming down.

Then Bird made me try a method grab. Yeah, *right*. But I tried it. I didn't do it, but I tried.

And that's what skateboarding is all about. Trying something new, really going all out for something you want. Something that looks impossible. Pumping for that bit of extra speed and force.

Maybe that's what life is all about, too.

*   *   *

The next week, Ryan rushed over to my house. He had the local paper in his hand.

"We won!" he shouted. "We won!"

I grabbed the paper. "Skateboarding Park Gets

Green Light," said the headline. Underneath was a picture of John and me at the meeting. Down below was a picture of Bird flying through the air.

"Yes!" I shouted and pumped my fist.

We ran to tell all our friends. My mom ordered pizza and we all ate outside in the backyard. I was so excited, I knew I wouldn't sleep that night. But that was okay. Mrs. Harris was having a party next door. It was really noisy. At one o'clock I was still wide awake, listening to loud music.

There's a bylaw that says no loud noise after eleven o'clock. For a while, I thought about calling the cops to complain. Then I thought about my mom and how she would say, 'live and let live'.

So I let it go. We've got our park. Mrs. Harris can have her party.

Sharon Jennings is the author of more than fifteen books for young people. Her first books for High Interest Publishing were the 'Bat Series:' *Bats Past Midnight* and *Bats in the Graveyard.*

Sharon says, "There is nothing I like to do more than write. I become the characters and live inside their story." In real life, Sharon Jennings balances her writing life with being a mother to two sons who skateboard and a daughter who dances. She lives in Toronto but frequently visits schools across Canada and in the United States. For more information, visit her website at www.sharon jennings.ca.